Danny's Great Goal

by

Michael Hardcastle

Illustrated by Martin Orme

To all aspiring footballers - keep
reading, keep playing

First published in Great Britain by Barrington Stoke Ltd
10 Belford Terrace, Edinburgh, EH4 3DQ
Copyright © 1999 Michael Hardcastle
Illustrations © Martin Orme
The moral right of the author has been asserted in
accordance with the Copyright, Designs and
Patents Act 1988
ISBN 1-902260-32-5
Printed by Polestar AUP Aberdeen Ltd

MEET THE AUTHOR - Michael Hardcastle

What is your favourite animal?
Polar bear
What is your favourite boy's name?
Robert
What is your favourite girl's name?
Romilly
What is your favourite food?
Smoked salmon
What is your favourite music?
Almost anything by Mozart or
Dvořák
What is your favourite hobby?
Playing table tennis

MEET THE ILLUSTRATOR - Martin Orme

What is your favourite animal?
Giraffe
What is your favourite boy's name?
James
What is your favourite girl's name?
Yasmin
What is your favourite food?
Thai
What is your favourite music?
Soul
What is your favourite hobby?
Skiing

Barrington Stoke was a famous and much-loved story-teller. He travelled from village to village carrying a lantern to light his way. He arrived as it grew dark and when the young boys and girls of the village saw the glow of his lantern, they hurried to the central meeting place. They were full of excitement and expectation, for his stories were always wonderful.

Then Barrington Stoke set down his lantern. In the flickering light the listeners were enthralled by his tales of adventure, horror and mystery. He knew exactly what they liked best and he loved telling a good story. And another. And then another. When the lantern burned low and dawn was nearly breaking, he slipped away. He was gone by morning, only to appear the next day in some other village to tell the next story.

Contents

Chapter 1
Danny's First Chance

Danny had promised himself that one day he would score that one goal in a million. Everyone would talk about it and he'd be famous. He'd join one of the world's top teams and he'd sign autographs for every single one of his army of fans.

He was dragged back to real life by Gary Almer, the coach of Gun Lane Shooters.

"Get yourself warmed up, Danny," Gary ordered. "Looks to me as if Colin's suffering a bit. Maybe it's that kick on his knee. Can't take risks with only ten minutes left."

Danny could feel his heart pumping overtime with excitement. At last he was getting into the action! At last he had a chance of scoring the sort of goal that would clinch his place in the Shooters' team for the Cup Final.

As Colin hobbled off, the coach told Danny what role he had to play. "I'm moving Stuart up front, so I need you to fill in for him at the back. Just ..."

"But I'm an *attacker*," Danny pointed out.

"Not now you're not," Gary Almer said firmly. "I want you to defend, defend as if your life depended on it. Defending's the important thing when you're one goal up in a semifinal.

It's important to keep it that way. So no forward runs from you, Danny."

Before this match started, Claxby had been the favourites to win the Cup. Now it looked as though they were going out before they could even reach the Cup Final. So they were attacking like a tornado, desperate for the equaliser to save this game.

For the first minute he was on the pitch, Danny never touched the ball. He knew he must obey the coach's orders, so he didn't dare go in search of it. He was playing in the semifinal at last, but was he going to get even one touch of the ball?

Then, without warning, one of his team-mates sliced a clearance and the ball shot towards Danny. With his left foot he just managed to control it. Then, with his right foot, he hit a perfect pass to Vince, the Shooters' captain and chief striker. But in the

second that Danny struck the ball, an opponent clattered into him from behind and sent him flying. He fell clumsily and felt the pain in his knee immediately. It was bad enough to bring tears to his eyes.

Gary Almer rushed onto the pitch to attend to Danny. The referee took the offender aside and gave him a stern warning. He had already been booked once. The referee finished by flourishing the red card. Danny's opponent was sent off for an illegal tackle.

"Think you can keep going, Danny boy?" the coach inquired, as he attended to the injury behind the knee.

"Er yes, I expect so," replied Danny, though he wasn't sure at all. The painkilling spray hadn't killed much pain yet.

"Well, you've helped a lot already," the coach told him. "The other lot are down to ten players. And I think that sending-off has finished 'em off."

For the remainder of the semifinal, Danny couldn't do much more than limp. Luckily, all he had to do, twice, was to head the ball. That was all right because usually he was confident about his heading ability.

When the final whistle sounded, Gun Lane Shooters had reached the Cup Final. He forgot about his aching leg and joined in the leaps and hugs and excitement of the celebrations. Every player was thinking about winning medals and glory and the Cup itself.

"Will I be in the team for the Cup Final, Mr Almer?" Danny wanted to know when he could get his attention.

Gary Almer shrugged. "Who can tell, Danny? Anything can happen to anybody, even to me! Nobody's got a firm promise of a place. Well, except for Vince, our captain. It's a very heavy cup and so we need a big lad like him to lift it for us! Anyway, Danny, keep your fingers crossed, never lose hope!"

Chapter 2
Cup Final Dreams

Danny found it hard to sleep that night.
Even when he tried to think of something else
his mind returned to his chances of playing in
the Cup Final against Silver Moor Stars.
Although he was sure his leg injury would clear
up he feared the coach might use it as an
excuse to drop him. After all, he'd only been a
sub in the semifinal. Yet Danny was certain
that if only the coach would pick him more
often he'd *prove* he was a player with a big

future, a player who'd *always* score goals. After all, he was the second leading scorer for his school team.

He woke early after a poor night. So that he could test his knee, he got out of bed immediately and moved up and down on his toes. The pain had gone! Well, almost. There was a bit of a twinge now and then. But maybe he could run that off.

He crept downstairs without making a sound. From the cupboard by the kitchen he took his football. The back door squeaked terribly and he paused to listen for any sounds from upstairs. Silence. Thankful, he closed the door and jogged towards Green Park. Every time he passed a solid gatepost he flicked the ball against it and then tried to make sure he trapped the rebound.

Just as he was about to cross the road by the entrance to the park, he spotted a familiar figure wheeling his bike down a garden path.

"Hey, Rich, good to see you," he called to Richard, one of his team-mates in the Shooters' squad. "Why don't you forget your paper deliveries and have a kick about?"

"No chance," was the gloomy reply. "I'm late already. Didn't sleep well last night because I had some really bad news."

Danny asked what was wrong.

"Going skiing with my family. Week after next. Can't get out of it because it's a prize for the whole family. Mum won a competition."

"Oh, so does that mean you'll miss the Cup Final?"

"Definitely. I tried pleading with Mum to let me stay behind, tried so hard I nearly lost my voice. But she won't give in. Worst day of my life, this is."

Richard was just about to pedal away to his next delivery when Danny said, "Just hang on a sec, Rich. Listen, if you can't play will you do something for me? Something really important. Could you tell Gary I should take your place in the team? Tell him I'm your best replacement. He'll listen to you because he likes you. Please?"

Richard frowned. "Oh, you don't need me to say anything. Anyway, Gary isn't going to do me any favours now. I had to give him my news last night and he says I've let the side down."

That was a blow to Danny's hopes. It hadn't occurred to him that Richard would have spoken to Gary Almer. Still, he needed any help he could to win a place in the Shooters' Cup Final line-up.

"Well, just say something, *please*. It just might work."

Richard was already back in the saddle after pulling a newspaper from the bag slung over his shoulder.

"See you, Dan," he called. He had made no promise of any kind.

Danny was both disappointed and hopeful at the same time. The important thing was that a gap now existed in the Shooters' midfield. He had to make sure he was the player to fill it. So he darted into the park, the ball at his feet. He was eager to practise some of his skills against the shooting wall which stood beside the children's play area.

Soon he was picking up the rebounds from the wall, which provided lots of different angles. Danny was thinking about his football heroes. They could trap a ball with one touch.

His favourite player was Albion's Italian star, Gino Salvini. Best of all, Danny liked his ability to use either foot with equal skill. One day Danny hoped to match his goal-scoring records.

After half-an-hour's hard work on the ball he realised he was hungry. When he looked at his watch he was astonished to see how late it was. If he didn't go home now he might miss

out on breakfast, because it would be time for
school.

To his surprise his Mum didn't seem to have
missed him. When he said he'd gone out early to
get fit she just nodded and said "Glad to hear it".

He guessed from her mood that she was
thinking about other things and he was right.
So he could enjoy his breakfast and dream
about the Cup Final in peace.

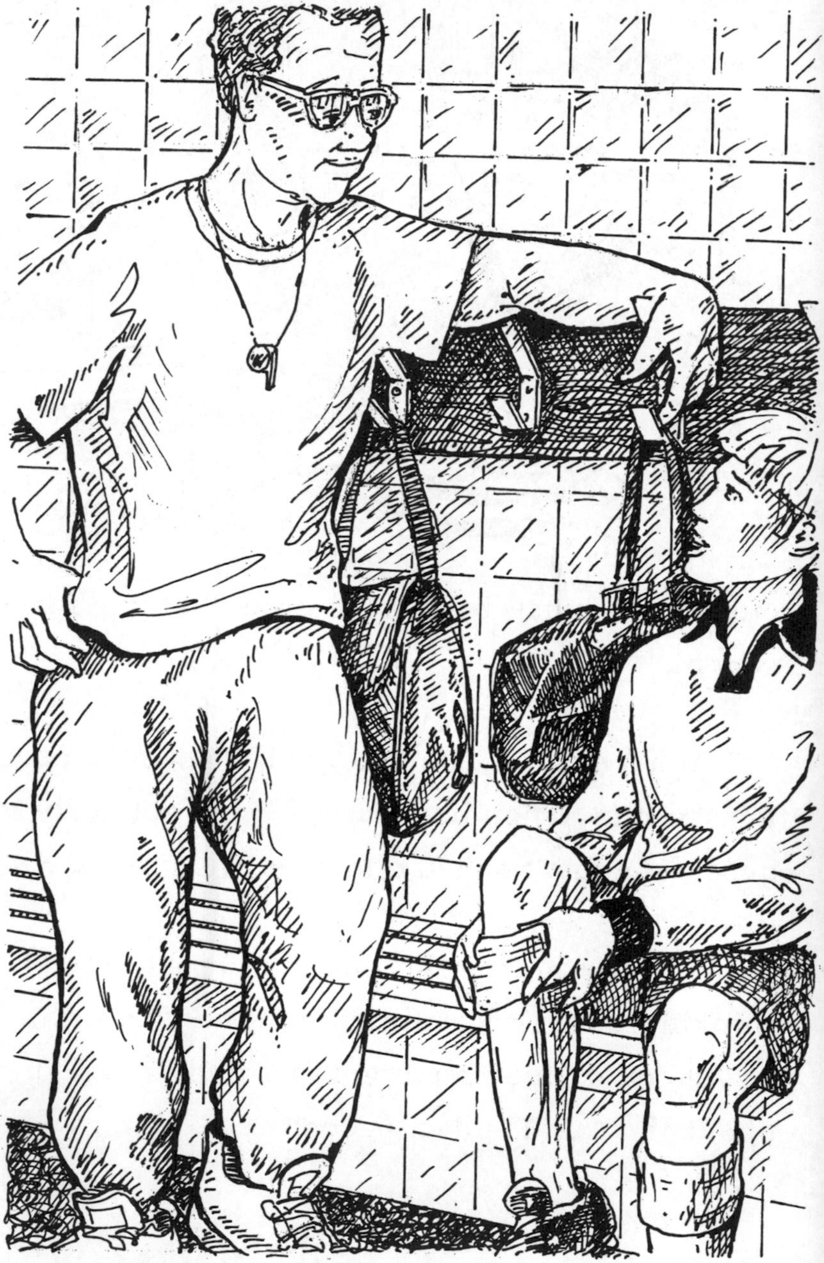

Chapter 3
A Tricky Situation

Two weeks later Danny surprised his sports teacher, Mr Lee. He was about to play for his own school team, Cavendish, against Bonham High.

"I think I should play as a defender today, Mr Lee," he announced, just before the teams went out on to the pitch.

Mr Lee couldn't hide his amazement.

"But you love scoring goals, Danny. I thought your heart was set on becoming the best goal scorer of all time."

"Well, yes," Danny agreed, "but I think I'll be a better attacker if I've got experience as a defender."

He didn't explain that this was Gary Almer's idea when coaching the Shooters. And he didn't mention that any experience of defending in the school team might be useful when he played in the Cup Final the next day.

"We might try that sometime, but not today," Mr Lee decided. "I want us to score a hatful of goals against Bonham High. Remember, they beat us at their place and I want revenge. Danny, I need you to throw yourself into this game, as you always do. Throw yourself about like mad. You'll make things happen. You're good at that."

Mr Lee didn't say a word about any skills Danny might possess. But then, he wasn't sure Danny possessed many ball-playing touches. In his view, Danny was a bit clumsy. What he really possessed was the energy of a monkey and the heart of a lion. Those were important qualities for any team.

Danny knew when he'd lost. Coaches and sports teachers, he reflected, always wanted things done their way.

He sighed. "OK, Mr Lee, I'll do my best to get us some goals."

Mr Lee patted him on the back. "Good lad. That's the spirit. Remember this, though – it's very wet out there after all this rain. So don't use up too much energy rushing all over the place. When you've got the ball, go direct for goal."

Just as they were about to step on to the pitch, Mohammed came across for a whispered word with his team-mate. Danny and he both played for the Shooters and for Cavendish School.

"You didn't say anything about the Cup Final tomorrow, did you, Danny? We don't want Gary to get to hear about us playing another match today."

Danny shook his head. "Definitely not. It's just our secret, Mo."

Mohammed was about the smallest player in the Cavendish School team and easily the fastest. He had astonishing speed from a standing start. He'd set up many goal-scoring chances for the grateful Danny who was now hoping there might be some more today.

Bonham High set off at a gallop. They seemed to believe they could win this game as easily as the one they'd won at home. Danny hardly saw the ball for the first few minutes because of their constant attacks.

Then, at last, Mohammed received a pass in space and flew down the wing, the driest part of the entire pitch. Danny was eager to get on to the cross that he knew Mo would aim at him. He charged into the Bonham penalty area. Few defenders were present and the goalkeeper, seeing real danger, came out. At the very last

moment the ball was caught by a gust of wind as it floated into the box and was carried out of play.

But it was too late for Danny to stop. When he tried to brake, his feet slipped from under him on the greasy surface. He and the goalkeeper collided and Danny felt a fearful crack on the side of his head from the goalkeeper's bony knee.

For some moments he just lay still and when he tried to get to his feet he was dizzy. He put his hand up to his head and there was blood on his fingers. Moments later Mr Lee was helping him from the pitch, murmuring that he was going to be all right.

"That's the end of the match for you, Danny boy," he said. "Can't take any risks after a knock on the head. But you were very brave. You always are. Don't worry, we'll soon have you fit again."

Mr Lee rummaged in his medical bag and then applied a bandage to the head wound. All Danny could think about was next day's Cup Final. He *had* to play in that. Then Mr Lee announced he'd find someone to take Danny home to make sure he could be looked after properly. By now the dizziness had gone and there was just a faint headache. When Mr Lee went to talk to spectators with cars, Danny seized his chance to talk to Mohammed.

"Mo, promise me you won't tell anyone about this," he begged, pointing to the bandage. "I'm going to play in the Cup Final whatever happens. Promise?"

"Well, yes," Mo replied, looking surprised. "If that's what you want. But everyone will see what you did, won't they?"

"I'll find a way out of that," said Danny with a confidence he didn't quite feel.

Chapter 4
Disaster

The next morning Danny could feel no ill effects from his bump on the head and he removed the bandage before going down for breakfast. All the same, he worried about what his Mum might say, for there were still faint graze marks on the skin.

"Are you *sure* you feel all right?" she pressed him. "You don't look it to me. Frankly, you look about half-dead! At your age you should be enjoying life, not collecting bruises from footie games."

"I'm fine," Danny insisted. "Just got things on my mind, that's all. Well, one thing – playing in the Cup Final means everything to me, Mum. You said I looked half-dead. Well, the other half of me will die if I don't play!"

She studied him closely, trying to make up her mind what to do. "I suppose we could put some of that special plaster over your graze, the stuff that allows the skin to breathe. Then ..."

"No, no, Mum, I don't need anything. If Gary Almer sees ..."

"Don't panic," she cut in. "It's colourless, nobody will notice anything. It's either that or you don't leave this house this morning. Make a quick decision, Daniel."

Danny knew she wasn't kidding.

"Well, please make the patch as small as possible, Mum."

When Danny left to go to the match on his bike, he was wondering whether Mohammed had told anyone about the injury in the school match. The previous evening his Mum hadn't allowed him to phone anyone, because she said he'd had enough excitement for one day. And no one had phoned him.

Gary Almer had given the Shooters their instructions at the training session, although he refused to name the team for the Cup Final.

"Got to keep my options open," he'd declared.

That, of course, had left Danny with plenty to worry about. Would he start the game, be left on the subs' bench or be left out altogether?

As he skidded round a tree trunk and into Orchard Lane Football Ground where the Cup Final was to be played, he suddenly felt a twinge of pain in his forehead. It was the first since the collision in the school game but it was gone next instant. All the same, it made him think about the Cup Final. Should he avoid going for a header? But he guessed the coach would notice what he was up to – Gary Almer missed nothing. No, he'd just have to hope for the best. Lots of people reported that they had much worse headaches than his and five minutes later they were perfectly all right.

Of course, Gary Almer noticed the plaster even though it was almost invisible.

"How'd you get that, Danny boy?"

"Er, just bumped into someone. Wasn't looking where I was going." This was the answer he'd prepared in case he needed it. It wasn't the complete truth, but it wasn't a lie, either.

"Better look where you're going when you play today, then," was Gary Almer's mild reaction. But then, he had more important matters on his mind. Danny let out a long breath – he'd got away with it! What's more he'd learned that he *was* in the team.

While they were changing into their maroon and white shirts and black shorts, Danny asked Mohammed, "You didn't say anything, did you?"

Mohammed grinned. "Not a word."

"Thanks, Mo, you're my mate for life," said Danny, slapping him on the back.

Before the team trotted out on to the pitch in heavy rain to face Silver Moor Stars, Gary Almer had a final word with Danny.

"Remember, you're not a striker now. You're a ball-winner in our defence. Your job is to get hold of the ball. If we don't have it, we can't play, can we? Don't be afraid of anything."

Vince had his own instructions to pass on to Danny as they took part in a kick around before the ref called for the teams to line up. "Your job is to get the ball to me, OK? Fast as you can,

right to my feet. I'll do the rest. That way we'll score loads of goals and win this match."

Danny knew that he had to please both Gary and Vince. If he let either of them down, then his place in the team might be lost for ever. After all, Richard would be back in time for the next match.

As the game kicked off, Danny was thinking that a Cup Final was the perfect stage on which to score his goal in a million. Even though he was playing at the back, there might be a chance to go upfield and try something special. After all, in such wet conditions a surprise shot from long-range could be a winner. Goalkeepers hated to deal with a greasy ball or one that skidded off a muddy surface.

Silver Moor Stars tested the Shooters' keeper, right from the start. But he was equal to anything they tried. So, in a different way, was Danny. He was determined to impress Gary

Almer with his skills. So he threw himself keenly into every aspect of the game – tackling, heading, intercepting and whacking the ball in Vince's direction whenever he won it.

Danny never gave a second thought to yesterday's knock on the head. Most of the time he succeeded in doing what he intended but he made some blunders – he misjudged the timing of a tackle or hit passes too short on the clinging surface.

"Calm it, Danny, calm it," Gary Almer called to him, after a fairly wild tackle brought a finger-wagging from the referee.

It was the last voice Danny heard for a little while. Suddenly, he was involved in another keen struggle for the ball. It had bounced high on probably the only dry patch on the pitch. Danny leapt for the ball but he didn't see his opponent, who was equally desperate for possession.

Just as Danny came down after missing the ball, his opponent's forehead caught Danny a glancing blow on the side of the head. Both players crashed to the ground. And Danny was the one who didn't get up again. He was out cold.

Some moments passed before the ref realised that Danny's injury was serious. Then, frantically, he signalled for help. Silver Moor Stars' coach saw that medical aid was needed. Within minutes a spectator was using his mobile phone to call an ambulance. Seven minutes later, Danny was on his way to hospital.

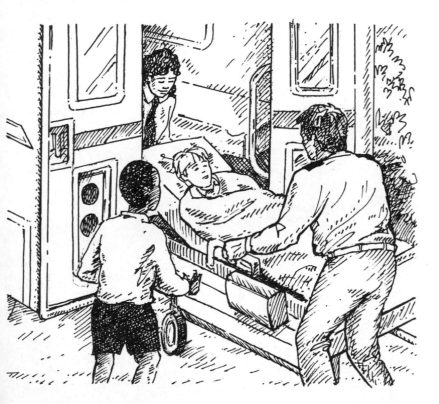

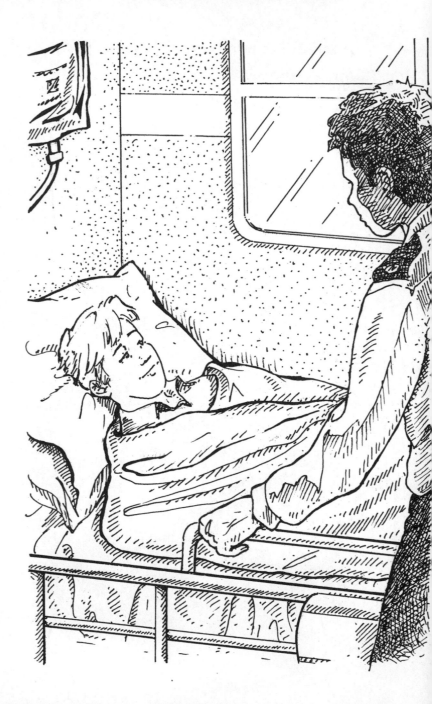

Chapter 5
Danny Meets his Hero

Danny woke soon after the ambulance set off, its blue light flashing. He wasn't sure where he was and he wasn't even sure how he felt. That's what he told the ambulance man who asked him.

"Well, you look OK to me, Danny," the man said in a gentle voice. "We're just nipping you off to hospital to check you out. They'll run a few tests on you, I expect."

That was exactly what happened. The doctor looked into his eyes with lights and asked him to watch things moving in front of him. Soon Danny was feeling perfectly normal.

When his Mum turned up, looking very upset, the doctor said, "Danny must stay in overnight for observation. That way we can see if there's any delayed reaction to his knock on the head. The tests didn't show up any problems, so we think he'll be as right as rain in the morning."

The moment his Mum stopped discussing his health, Danny asked her about the Cup Final. "Did we win?"

She was shaking her head until she saw the horror on his face.

"No, but you didn't lose, either. The referee called it off in the second half because the pitch was unplayable after so much rain. Well, that's what Mr Almer told me when he rang. It seems it'll have to be played again but ..."

"When?" Danny asked, worried.

"Oh, don't ask me that! I've no idea and I don't suppose anyone else has at present. Listen, I've got to go now. I'll be back later. So just relax – and do as the nurses tell you!"

Danny's mind was already racing through the possibilities for the new date for the Cup Final. Would the coach blame him for his accident? After all, he hadn't told the whole truth about how he got that graze on his head yesterday. Was it really only yesterday?

Gary Almer might say he'd let the Shooters down by getting injured twice in two days. If Mohammed broke his promise and told how Danny had been injured in the school match, then even the other players might feel he was at fault.

Another thought struck him. If the Cup Final couldn't be replayed for a week or more, then Richard would be back, eager to reclaim his place in the side. Gary Almer would probably give it to him, too, because he'd played in most games that season.

"Cheer up, youngster, nothing's as bad as you think," said a voice from the next bed. "You don't look poorly to me, so what are you worrying about?"

"Football," Danny replied.

"Do you play, then?"

"Of course. That's how I got injured."

"Well, you're in good company in here, then," remarked the elderly man in blue-striped pyjamas.

"What do you mean?" Danny wanted to know.

"Well, there's a professional footballer who's a patient here – Italian, I think, plays for Albion. Had some minor operation, I believe."

Danny didn't have any doubt who it must be.

"Gino Salvini!" he exclaimed. "Albion's Italian star player. In this hospital, like me? Wow!"

He was awe-struck.

"Yes, that'll be him," the elderly man confirmed. "Why, do you know him, then?"

"No, but I'm going to get his autograph. Do you know which room he's in?"

"I believe it's a private room, just off Ward D. I'm sure any nurse will show you where it is. They all seem to drool over him, like you're doing."

Danny slipped out of bed and was about to dash out of the ward when the elderly man called, "Hang on! You can't walk around like that. Folk will think you're on the run. Take my dressing gown. I'm a small chap so I reckon it'll fit you a treat. Then you'll look as if you belong."

"Thanks, Mr –"

"Allen. Tommy Allen. Off you go."

Chapter 6
Some Expert Advice

When he passed a nurse in the long corridor she just smiled at him, so Danny was confident he wouldn't run into any trouble. He realised, too, that he felt perfectly well – no dizziness, no aches or pains. He felt normal. So when the doctors came to look at him again they'd probably say he could go home right away. This might be his only chance therefore, to meet his hero.

Then he spotted Gino Salvini through a partly open door.

"Hey, who are you?" was the friendly greeting.

Danny had no difficulty in recognising the man with the mass of curly black hair and the beak-like nose, even though he was dressed in a white top and lying in bed.

"Er, I'm a fan, come to get your autograph – *please*." Danny told him.

"And a patient, too, dressed like that, I think. Yes?"

"Oh yes. Just got a knock on the head playing football. But ..."

"Listen, can you do something for me? You arrived at just the right time."

"Anything," said Danny. He was amazed to be asked such a question.

"I need a coffee. Nurse Angela, she makes divine coffee. But I can't seem to catch her. The nurses have a little kitchen just up the corridor, on the left. Ask for one of her specials. They know I love coffee. They'll give you one also if you like. OK?"

He was in luck. Nurse Angela was in the kitchen, actually making coffee for someone else.

When Danny delivered Gino's message she grinned and said, "He can have his coffee, but I'm afraid I'm too busy to take it to him. He always wants to chat to me for ages! I do have other patients to look after."

So Danny took the mug and set off down the passage.

"Fantastic!" Gino greeted Danny as he arrived with the coffee. He started sipping it immediately. Then he gave Danny a puzzled look.

"Aren't you having one?"

"Er, I forgot to ask the nurse."

"You like to share mine?" Gino asked.

Danny was tempted, but shook his head. Somehow it was hard to believe that a world famous footballer was offering to share his mug of coffee with a hero-worshipping boy he'd only just met.

Then they started talking about football. Danny had to give details of his teams and why he was in hospital and what he wanted most to do in life. He found it easy to tell him everything, because Gino was such a good listener. Gino seemed really interested in everything he heard and it never occurred to Danny that Gino might be lonely. When he asked about any weaknesses in Danny's play, he showed no signs of boredom.

"Maybe I can help you there, Danny," he said. "Maybe you and I can do a little training together. I may be able to show you – how do you say it? – a few tricks."

"That would be fantastic!" Danny gasped. "When?"

"I should be out of this place tomorrow. You, too, I think. Then I need to build up my knee again with light training. So, the day after tomorrow, eh?"

"But why would you do this for me, Gino? I mean, why *me*?"

"You did something for me, I do something for you?"

"All I did was fetch you a mug of coffee."

Gino smiled his most dazzling smile.

"Danny, a coffee can save a man's life!"

Before Danny could say another word a nurse came in, wagged a finger at him like a ref and complained, "I've been looking for you, young man. The doctor wants to see you and you should have been in your bed. Now, get off back to your ward before I stick a needle in you!"

"Bye, Danny. See you soon for our training," Gino called as Danny darted away.

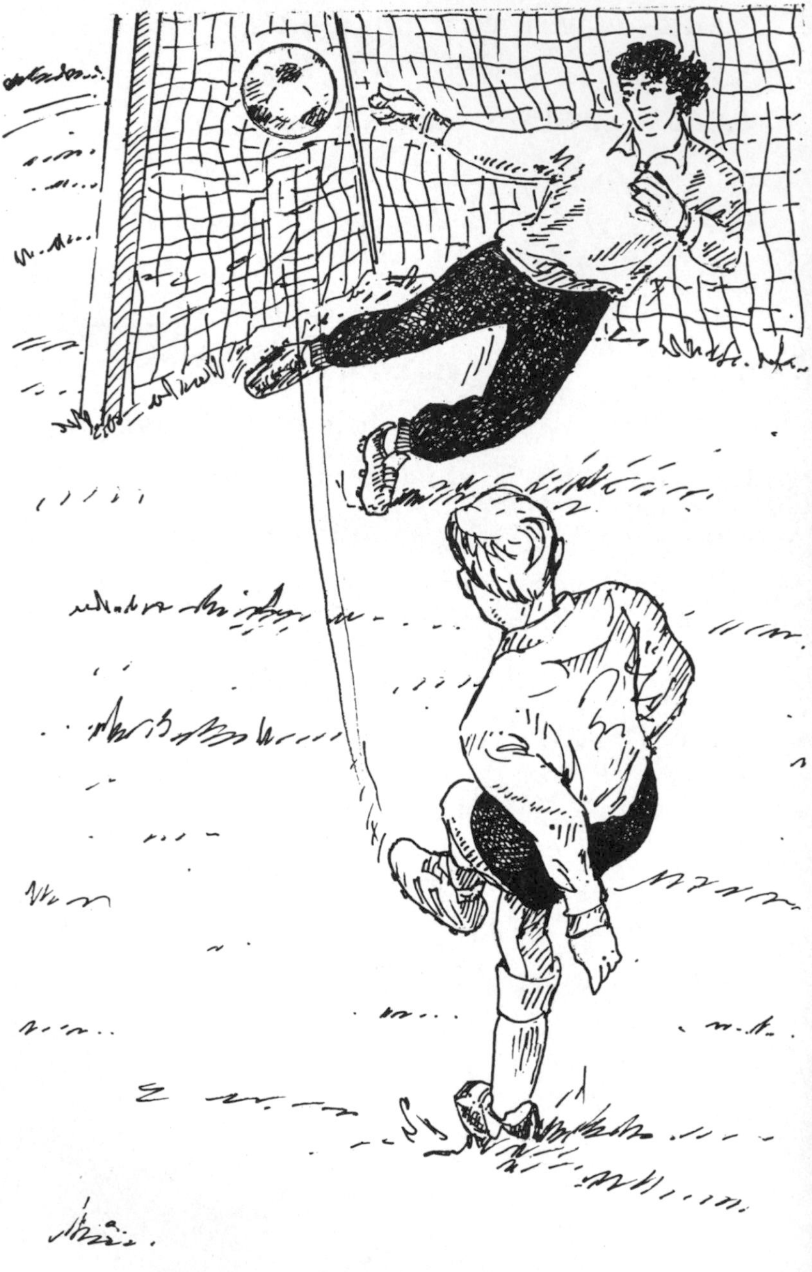

Chapter 7
A Stroke of Luck

Gino had been coaching Danny for a week. Danny flicked the ball up with his right foot, then swivelled round. With his left foot, he hit a shot that sent the ball flying past Gino's shoulder and into the net. He raised his arms in delight and yelled, "Goal!"

Gino grinned and held up his left thumb.

"Very, very good, Danny, You have learned much this week. You are an excellent pupil. But now we stop. My leg aches a little. Maybe I have trained too much. Anyway, it is time to go home."

Danny still found it hard to believe that the Italian had been willing to spend so much time with him since they'd left hospital. But Gino said he wanted to be a coach when his playing days ended and so he might as well start now, with Danny as his first pupil.

They'd talked about the delayed Cup Final and Danny's worries about getting back into the Shooters' team. After all, he'd never told Gary Almer the whole truth about his first head injury.

"It's not important," Gino said. "We all do it, we all hide things from the boss to keep our place in the team. I'm sure you'll play in the Final on Sunday."

"Well, he told me last night I seem to have improved. So I've got my fingers crossed. I'll be in if there's room for me!"

"And I'll be there to watch you, Danny. So put on a great show for me," Gino added.

*****

It was only when he was almost home that Danny knew he was actually going to play. For there was Richard, slowly making his way along the pavement, his left leg in plaster.

Danny didn't have a chance to speak before Richard growled, "Don't say it! I did break it skiing, but it wasn't my fault because some idiot ran into me. And now I find the Cup Final's still to be played. Of all the rotten luck ..."

"Rich, I'm really sorry for you," Danny said. But he couldn't help thinking that his own luck was *really* in!

Chapter 8
Goal!

Dozens of photographers were snapping pictures for local papers and family albums as the Cup Final teams ran out on to the sunny pitch.

Soon the captains were shaking hands and exchanging gifts in the team colours. Danny glanced round the ring of spectators. His parents were there, waving wildly. Sadly, there

was no sign yet of Gino, but he hadn't promised he would be there for the kick off.

Danny was playing at the back again because, the coach had told him, he was showing a lot of promise as a defender.

"Cup Finals are won by good defending as well as good attacking," Gary Almer had said in the team talk a few minutes earlier. "So, Danny, make the position your own. Don't make forward runs. Defend as if your life depended on it!"

With their supporters cheering madly and many waving maroon and white flags, Gun Lane Shooters started at a hectic pace. Vince, the Shooters' captain, displayed excellent dribbling skills. He wove his way through the opposition. First he, and then Patrick, fired in fierce shots only for the Silver Moor goalie to bring off confident saves.

Then Vince began switching the attack from himself to the speedy Mohammed, and then back to Patrick. For the first quarter of the match the Silver Moor Stars weren't able to get the ball out of their own half.

Yet the Stars didn't concede a goal. Their defence hadn't been beaten for seven matches on the run and it wasn't hard to see why. They knew how to tackle and clear their lines. Their goalie was outstanding, alert and athletic and brave enough to dive headlong into a scrum of kicking boots to grab the ball.

Danny desperately wanted to join the attack. But after crossing the halfway line once and getting an angry word from Gary Almer, he decided he'd better stay back. If he made a bad mistake, the coach might put the sub on in his place and that would be the end of all his dreams.

Gradually, the Stars began to press forward. They'd soaked up the Shooters' pressure without crumbling. Now they launched their own attacks. Danny found himself having regular battles with a thin, blond-haired striker who knew plenty of tricks. But Danny stuck with him and at half-time there was still no score.

"Just keep playing as you are doing," Gary Almer instructed his team as they sipped fruit drinks and ate energy bars at half-time. "I'm sure we'll break them down soon."

Yet when the game started again the deadlock remained. Now the ball was swinging from one to the other. Both goalies were inspired and no one could find a way to outwit them. Shots on target from any range were gathered cleanly and easily. Other players were getting tired and mistakes were creeping in.

Danny guessed that his coach might put a sub on at any time. But who would he take off? Well, it might be him. So if the game went into extra time he'd have to sit it out in agony as a mere spectator.

"Come on, Stars, you can win it!" a supporter was yelling close to Danny.

Then Danny saw why he was so excited. The blond attacker was running towards him with the ball. Danny went for him. His tackle was perfectly timed as he slid in for the ball and took it away from his opponent. The Stars' player stumbled and sat down and simply couldn't find the energy to get up again.

Danny, unchallenged, ran into the heart of the opposition. He could see no one in a good position to pass to. Not expecting him to keep going so long, the Silver Moor defence fell back, and back, and back.

"Go for goal, Danny!" someone yelled, and Danny recognised that voice. Gino Salvini. So he was here after all!

Now he had a clear sight of goal. Not for a split second did he think of passing to Vince, who was screaming for the ball. Instead, he looked up once and then, with all his power, fired in a shot.

The goalie was already advancing to narrow the angle of attack. He was helpless to stop the ball as it flew over his head. But it was just too high to enter the net. Instead, it rebounded from the shuddering crossbar.

But Danny hadn't stopped running. With the goalie still trying to scramble back into position, Danny skipped round him. He skilfully controlled the ball and calmly steered it into the net for the only goal of the game.

"What a goal!" yelled Vince as he rushed to hug Danny along with the rest of the team. Danny could see that Gino was clapping with his hands high above his head. He wanted to go and thank the Italian star, but this wasn't the moment to do it.

In spite of feeling totally thrilled with his success, he still wondered what Gary Almer would say as the teams came off the pitch to

collect their medals and the Cup. But he needn't
have worried.

"Greatest bit of defending I've ever seen,
Danny boy!" exclaimed the coach, laughing
happily.

But no one was happier than Danny.

Other Barrington Stoke titles available:-

What's Going On, Gus? by Jill Atkins 1-902260-10-4
Nicked! by David Belbin 1-902260-29-5
Bungee Hero by Julie Bertagna 1-902260-23-6
Hostage by Malorie Blackman 1-902260-12-0
The Two Jacks by Tony Bradman 1-902260-30-9
Starship Rescue by Theresa Breslin 1-902260-24-4
Ghost for Sale by Terry Deary 1-902260-14-7
Sam the Detective by Terrance Dicks 1-902260-19-8
Billy the Squid by Colin Dowland 1-902260-04-X
Eddie and the Zedlines by Colin Dowland 1-902260-31-7
Kick Back by Vivian French 1-902260-02-3
The Gingerbread House by Adèle Geras 1-902260-03-1
Ship of Ghosts by Nigel Hinton 1-902260-33-3
Virtual Friend by Mary Hoffman 1-902260-00-7
The Genie by Mary Hooper 1-902260-20-1
Tod in Biker City by Anthony Masters 1-902260-15-5
Wartman by Michael Morpurgo 1-902260-05-8
Whirlwind by Judith O'Neill 1-902260-34-1
Extra Time by Jenny Oldfield 1-902260-13-9
Screw Loose by Alison Prince 1-902260-01-5
Life Line by Rosie Rushton -902260-21-X
Problems with a Python by Jeremy Strong 1-902260-22-8
Lift Off by Hazel Townson 1-902260-11-2

Barrington Stoke, 10 Belford Terrace, Edinburgh EH4 3DQ
Tel: 0131 315 4933 Fax: 0131 315 4934
E-mail: info@barringtonstoke.co.uk
Website: www.barringtonstoke.co.uk